MISS

Flame

Have you seen this kitten?

Flame is a magic kitten of royal blood, missing from his own world.
His uncle, Ebony, is very keen that he is found quickly.
Flame may be hard to spot as he often appears in a
variety of fluffy kitten colours but you can recognize him
by his big emerald eyes and whiskers that crackle with magic!

He is believed to be looking for a young friend to take care of him.

Could it be you?

If you find this very special kitten please let Ebony,
ruler of the Lion Throne, know.

MISSING!

Sue Bentley's books for children often include animals or fairies. She lives in Northampton and enjoys reading, going to the cinema, and sitting watching the frogs and newts in her garden pond. If she hadn't been a writer, she would probably have been a skydiver or a brain surgeon. The main reason she writes is that she can drink pots and pots of tea while she's typing. She has met and owned many cats and each one has brought a special sort of magic to her life.

Magic Kitten

A Circus Wish

SUE BENTLEY

Illustrated by Angela Swan

PUFFIN

To Lucky, the neighbourly black and white boy

PUFFIN BOOKS

Published by the Penguin Group
Penguin Books Ltd, 80 Strand, London WC2R ORL, England
Penguin Group (USA) Inc., 375 Hudson Street, New York, New York 10014, USA
Penguin Group (Canada), 90 Eglinton Avenue East, Suite 700, Toronto, Ontario, Canada M4P 2Y3
(a division of Pearson Penguin Canada Inc.)
Penguin Ireland, 25 St Stephen's Green, Dublin 2, Ireland (a division of Penguin Books Ltd)
Penguin Group (Australia), 250 Camberwell Road, Camberwell, Victoria 3124, Australia
(a division of Pearson Australia Group Pty Ltd)
Penguin Books India Pvt Ltd, 11 Community Centre, Panchsheel Park, New Delhi – 110 017, India
Penguin Group (NZ), 67 Apollo Drive, Mairangi Bay, Auckland 1310, New Zealand
(a division of Pearson New Zealand Ltd)
Penguin Books (South Africa) (Pty) Ltd, 24 Sturdee Avenue, Rosebank, Johannesburg 2196, South Africa

Penguin Books Ltd, Registered Offices: 80 Strand, London WC2R ORL, England

penguin.com

Published 2006
8

Text copyright © Susan Bentley, 2006
Illustrations copyright © Angela Swan, 2006
All rights reserved

The moral right of the author and illustrator has been asserted

Set in Bembo
Typeset by Palimpsest Book Production Limited, Grangemouth, Stirlingshire
Made and printed in England by Clays Ltd, St Ives plc

British Library Cataloguing in Publication Data
A CIP catalogue record for this book is available from the British Library

ISBN-13: 978-0-141-32154-7

www.greenpenguin.co.uk

Penguin Books is committed to a sustainable future
for our business, our readers and our planet.
The book in your hands is made from paper
certified by the Forest Stewardship Council.

Prologue

The young white lion's heart beat fast as he looked at the plains and distant mountains shimmering in the heat. All was quiet. He felt a surge of hope. Perhaps he need hide no longer.

Suddenly a deep roar split the air and an enormous black adult lion appeared, bounding towards him from the far shore.

'Ebony!' the young white lion gasped in fear.

Before he knew what was happening, there was a bright flash and a shower of silver sparkles. In the young white lion's place now crouched a tiny, fluffy coal-black kitten.

The kitten backed up slowly, trembling with fear as it scrambled into a clearing in nearby reeds, out of the black lion's sight.

There was a stealthy movement to one side and the reeds parted. An old grey lion emerged into the clearing and bowed its head before the kitten.

'Greetings, Prince Flame. I am glad to see you safe and well. But you have returned at a dangerous time,' he rumbled.

'Cirrus.' Flame greeted his old friend quietly. 'It seems that my uncle still rules my kingdom.'

'He does,' Cirrus replied gravely. 'And he has many spies looking for you. If Ebony kills you, there will be no one to stop his evil.'

Flame lifted his tiny chin and his big emerald eyes smouldered with anger. 'One day I will challenge him and take my rightful place on the Lion Throne!' he mewed bravely.

Cirrus nodded, his old muzzle wrinkling in a proud smile. 'But for now, you must leave. Use your disguise to hide far away and grow strong and wise.'

Another terrifying roar rang out. Flame peered through the reeds. He

glimpsed a big dark shape as it
bounded towards them.

'Go! Save yourself!' Cirrus urged.

There was another flash. And Flame
felt himself falling. Falling . . .

Chapter
ONE

Sadie Allen tensed as she ran forward
and jumped high in the air. Tucking
her head under, she flipped over and
landed with a soft thud of her bare
feet.

Sadie's classmates clapped and
whooped.

'Thank you, fans!' Sadie joked as she
performed a mock bow.

She really loved gymnastics and the
circus skills workshop at her school was
turning out to be something she was
really good at. First there had been the
warm-up games and now they had
moved on to floor acrobatics – it had
been the best fun ever!

'That was great, Sadie! Well done!'
called Lena.

Sadie tossed her long fair plait over her
shoulder and grinned at the older girl.

Lena Tomani was a circus performer who was appearing with her parents in their trapeze act at the nearby circus school. She had come to Sadie's school to demonstrate and share some of her skills.

Lena was tall for her twelve years and pretty, with short dark hair and a confident manner. Presto, her shaggy little dog, followed close at heel as Lena moved round the gym.

Lena turned to another girl. 'Off you go, Jenny. Don't try anything too complicated at first.'

Jenny Coleman was Sadie's best friend. They lived a few houses away from each other. 'Go for it!' Sadie called out to Jenny encouragingly.

Jenny screwed up her face in

concentration as she threw herself on to the mat. She curled into a forward roll, but her arms and legs shot out at angles and she collapsed into an untidy sprawl.

There was a ripple of laughter.

'Shut up, you lot!' Sadie defended her friend. She helped Jenny scramble to her feet. 'Are you all right?'

Jenny's round face was bright red and sweaty. 'Course I am! Leave me alone. You're just making it worse.'

'Sorry.' Sadie blushed and stood aside, as Jenny pushed past her off the exercise mat. She tried not to feel too hurt by Jenny's words. She just wished that her friend could enjoy the workshop as much as she did.

Lena and her little dog were going over to another group who were learning balancing skills. Some of the kids in the year above Sadie were walking on stilts and trying the unicycle. There was a lot of giggling going on.

'Sadie! Why don't you come and have a try at this?' Lena called. 'It's a bit more advanced, but you should be fine.'

'OK,' Sadie answered. She tugged at Jenny's arm. 'Why don't you come too?'

Jenny shook her head. 'You go. I don't suppose Lena wants any clumsy fairy elephants over there.'

'But you could just watch if you want. Lena won't mind.'

'I think I'll get a drink instead. I'll

see you later,' Jenny said. She wandered off towards the drinks machine.

Sadie hesitated. Should she go after Jenny? Her friend really didn't seem to be having fun at all.

'There's a set of stilts here if you're interested, Sadie!' Lena shouted.

Sadie made up her mind. 'OK. I'm coming!'

It was great fun stomping around on the stilts. Sadie had natural balance and found it easy to keep up with the older girls.

When it was time for a break, Miss Kemp, the gym teacher, called for everyone to gather together and sit in a circle. 'Lena's kindly offered to give us a demonstration of what can be achieved with discipline and hard work.'

Sadie went and sat down next to
Jenny. 'This should be good!' she
enthused.

Jenny shrugged. 'It'll probably just be
Lena showing off.'

'What's the matter? Don't you like
her?' Sadie looked at her friend in
surprise.

'I suppose she's OK,' Jenny replied.
'But she's hardly said a word to me.'

'That's only because you didn't join

in very much. Lena's been really friendly with everyone,' Sadie said.

'I don't know why you're sticking up for her,' Jenny murmured.

'I'm not . . .' Sadie began.

'Can we have silence, please,' Miss Kemp interrupted. 'Lena's ready now.'

Lena had now taken off her tracksuit to reveal a red leotard with gold braid at the neck and wrists. She made a graceful sweeping gesture with her arms, then bent over and went straight into a handstand.

Sadie watched with wide blue eyes as Lena did a standing backflip and then performed a series of high jumps with impossible twists and turns in mid-air. Her body seemed to flow from one movement to another. Lena finished

with another handstand and then
swung down and went into the splits.
She held the last movement, with her
hands curved elegantly overhead.

Presto, who had been watching
intently, ran over to his owner. Standing
up on his back legs and wagging his
tail, the little dog pirouetted in front of
Lena.

The gym erupted with applause.

Sadie clapped like mad. Lena was
fantastic. She would give anything to be
even half as good.

Lena uncurled. She stood up
gracefully and then picked up Presto,
who whined and licked her chin.
'Thank you. You are very kind. Presto
taught himself that trick. He loves to
perform with me just for fun.'

Miss Kemp
thanked Lena for
the workshop and
her demonstration.
'We've really
enjoyed learn-
ing some new
skills.'

There was more
applause and shouts of
agreement.

Lena smiled warmly
as she looked
round at all the
eager faces. 'I've
enjoyed meeting you all too. You might
like to know that there's a circus youth
club on weekdays, after school. There're
leaflets on the table near the door.

Anyone who's interested can put their names on the list.'

As Lena went off to change, there was a buzz of excitement. A few kids wandered over to the table and looked at the leaflets. Sadie dashed straight over and picked one up. She came back to Jenny with it.

'Circus youth club sounds great,' she said eagerly, scanning the leaflet. 'Shall we sign up?'

Jenny seemed unsure. 'I don't know. I'm rubbish at all that tumbling and balancing stuff.'

'That's OK. It says here that there's tons of other stuff to do. Like juggling, comedy skills and circus history just for a start. It'll be great fun!'

'Juggling?' Jenny's face brightened a

little for the first time that day. 'OK then. I don't mind giving youth club a try.'

As Sadie and Jenny were adding their names to the list, Lena came over with Presto trotting at her heels. 'I'm glad you'll be coming, Sadie. You've got a natural talent for acrobatics. Maybe you'll be a performer yourself one day,' she said with a warm smile.

Sadie beamed back. 'Thanks. But I'll never be as good as you are,' she said modestly.

Lena laughed. 'I have a head start, don't forget. I come from a circus family. Dad says that talent is useful, but hard work and dedication make a performer.' She looked down at Jenny and her voice softened kindly. 'He also says that everyone has a skill, but sometimes it takes a while to discover it.'

Jenny's round cheeks flushed deep pink. 'I reckon mine must be really well hidden!' she joked and then she turned to Sadie. 'Are you ready to go? I have to meet my mum.'

'OK. I'm coming. Bye!' Sadie called to Lena, hurrying towards the cloakroom after Jenny. 'See you at the youth club!'

On the way, she paused by a colourful poster advertising the circus. There was Lena in a close-fitting sparkling costume with the other Flying Tomanis, as they performed their trapeze act.

Sadie's imagination went into fast forward. She could smell the greasepaint, see her own name up in lights and hear the audience applauding as she tumbled through the air like magic!

Chapter
★ TWO ★

Sadie hurried after Jenny as her friend headed for the changing rooms. She had a tight knot of excitement in her stomach. 'Did you hear what Lena said? She thinks I've got talent!'

Jenny didn't look round. 'I heard her saying that to some other kids. I reckon she just wants to get loads of people to go to the youth club.'

Sadie's high spirits took a dent. 'Don't you think Lena meant it?' she asked anxiously.

Jenny looked back at Sadie quickly, her face flushed. 'Who cares . . .' She stopped suddenly and then just shrugged. 'Course she did.' She grinned. 'Race you to get changed!'

'You're on!' Sadie whipped off her T-shirt and gym shorts in double quick time.

Jenny was out of her gym kit and
into her school uniform in a jiffy. But
she lost time trying to stuff her feet
into her school shoes. Sadie was almost
dressed. She bent down as she pulled
on a sock, lost her balance and backed
into Jenny.

'Oops! Sorry!' she said, laughing as
they both staggered and almost fell
over.

'Hey – you hit me with your bottom
on purpose. You cheat!' Jenny shrieked.

Suddenly they both burst out
laughing. They sank on to the benches,
out of breath and clutching each other

'I call that a draw,' Sadie gasped,
holding her aching ribs.

'Suits me,' Jenny agreed, slinging her
gym bag over her shoulder. 'Come on.

We'll be late. Mum's waiting for me at the hairdresser's. I'm having my hair done as part of my present.'

It was Jenny's birthday next week. Sadie was planning to buy her a present with her pocket money.

'You lucky thing!' Sadie said enviously, fingering her long plait as they left the changing room. 'My mum usually just trims my ends for me.'

They were almost at the school gate before Sadie remembered something. 'Oh, no, I've left my schoolbooks in the cloakroom.'

'They'll be OK in there. You can get them tomorrow,' Jenny said.

Sadie chewed at her lip, undecided. 'I could. But I've got maths homework to finish. I really need one of the books. I might as well go and get them all.'

Jenny fidgeted, trying not to look impatient. 'Do you want me to come back with you?'

'No. You go on. I'll see you later.' She waved as Jenny went out of the gate and down the street.

Sadie sprinted back into school and hurried towards the gym. There was no one else around and the gym and cloakroom were dark and deserted. Her footsteps echoed eerily as she went to press the light switch. One row of strip lights flickered on, leaving the rest of the benches and clothes rails in deep shadows.

Sadie spotted her books lying in a pile where she'd left them. She bent down to pick them up when suddenly,

out of the corner of her eye, she saw a
flash of bright white light.

'Hello, is someone else in here?' Sadie
called, looking round.

No one answered. Sadie shivered –
this was really creepy. She gave herself a
shake and decided to stop being silly. It
must have been the caretaker, turning a
light on in one of the classrooms
outside. She was about to leave when
she saw something glowing faintly on a
nearby bench.

Puzzled, Sadie went forward slowly.
There on the bench, backed into the
very corner of the room, crouched a
tiny kitten. Its dark coat glittered with
thousands of tiny lights. Sadie blinked
hard. Had someone left a toy kitten
here?

As she got closer, the sparkles seemed to fade. The kitten was really lifelike, with glossy black fur and wide emerald-green eyes.

'You're really cute. I wonder who you belong to,' Sadie said aloud.

The kitten sat up. 'I belong to no one but myself,' it mewed.

Sadie's jaw dropped in total amazement. 'You can talk!' she gasped.

Her books slipped from her numb

fingers and dropped to the wooden
floor with a loud clatter.

'Mia-ow-ow!' screeched the kitten. It
shot into the air on stiff little legs, its
hackles raised.

'Sorry. I didn't mean to scare you. I
. . . I dropped my schoolbooks,' Sadie
stammered in complete shock.

She couldn't quite believe what was
happening, but she didn't want to scare
this amazing kitten away, so she bent
down and made herself as small as
possible.

The kitten's black fur all stood on
end, but Sadie could see the fear
starting to fade from its emerald-green
eyes. 'What is your name?' it asked in a
velvety miaow.

'I'm Sadie. Sadie Allen. I live nearby,'

Sadie said gently. 'Who are you?'

'I am Prince Flame,' replied the kitten proudly, lifting his pointed chin and sitting up straight. 'Heir to the Lion Throne.'

Sadie was having difficulty taking it all in. 'Did you say, *Lion* Throne?' she asked, looking doubtfully at his tiny fluffy body.

Flame didn't answer, but his black fur began to sparkle all over. He jumped to the floor and Sadie was blinded by a bright silver flash.

'Oh!' she rubbed her eyes. Sadie blinked hard and saw that in Flame's place now stood a majestic young white lion. She was awestruck. 'Flame?'

'Yes, Sadie. It is me,' Flame replied in a deep rumbling growl.

Then, just as Sadie began to get used
to the great white lion, there was
another flash of light and Flame
reappeared as a tiny coal-black kitten.

'Wow! You really are a lion prince,'
she whispered. 'No one would ever
know. That's a really convincing
disguise!'

Flame nodded. 'But my disguise will
not save me if my uncle finds me. Will
you hide me, Sadie? I am in danger!'

Sadie's heart went out to the tiny kitten. She scooped him up. 'Of course I will. But who did you say was after you?'

'My uncle Ebony. He has stolen my throne. He sends his spies to search for me. When they find me, they will kill me,' Flame mewed anxiously.

Sadie stroked his soft little head. 'Then we have to make sure they never find you. I'll take you home. You can live with –' She broke off suddenly.

Flame looked up into her face. 'Is there a problem, Sadie?'

'Sort of,' Sadie admitted. 'It's my dad. He's allergic to cats.'

'What is allergic?' Flame purred.

'It means when you have a weird reaction to something,' Sadie explained.

29

'Dad sneezes and his eyes water when he gets anywhere near cats. He's never going to let me keep you.'

Flame nodded. 'Very well, I understand. Thank you for your kindness, Sadie. I will find someone else who can help me.'

'No! Wait!' Sadie burst out. She really didn't want Flame to go.

She thought hard. There had to be some way to get round the problem. 'I know. I'll smuggle you into our house. You can live in my bedroom. Dad won't know you're there. This is great. I'm dying to tell Jenny about how you can talk and everything. Jenny's my best fr–'

She broke off as Flame placed his tiny black paws on her chest and looked up at her. 'You cannot tell anyone about my secret. Promise me, Sadie.'

As Sadie looked into his troubled emerald eyes, she felt a surge of affection for the tiny kitten. 'All right, Flame. I promise. You'll be my secret.'

'Thank you,' Flame purred softly, rubbing the top of his soft little head against her chin.

'I think it's time we went. Can you get in here?' Sadie opened her school bag, and Flame jumped inside. He settled straight down on top of her books and she heard him rumbling contentedly as she turned off the cloakroom lights and headed for home.

Chapter
* THREE *

The following morning Sadie woke
first thing with something tickling her
nose. As she went to brush it away, her
fingers felt a set of whiskers.

'Good morning,' Flame purred
happily into her ear.

'Flame!' It was her secret magic
kitten! He was really here, living in her
bedroom. Reaching for him, Sadie gave

him a cuddle. 'Did you sleep well?'

Flame snuggled his warm little body against her. 'Yes. Thank you. I feel safe here with you.'

Sadie thought she could have stayed there for hours, but she had agreed to meet Jenny at the shopping centre that morning and she knew that Flame must be hungry! Throwing back the duvet, she jumped out and dressed quickly. 'I'm going down for breakfast, but I'll be back soon with something for you to eat.'

Flame jumped across to the window and looked down at the garden.

'Be careful someone doesn't see you,' Sadie warned.

Flame turned to look at her. 'Do not worry. I will make myself invisible when I am in your house.'

'Really?' Sadie asked in surprise. 'You can do that?'

Flame nodded his little head.

'Well, in that case then, yes. I think that would be a good idea,' Sadie replied, grinning at the excitement of it all.

Sadie wolfed down her breakfast and smuggled a glass of milk up to Flame as quickly as she could. 'It's all I could get. I'll buy you some proper cat food with my pocket money,' she promised.

Flame purred as he drank his milk.

While he was washing his face, Sadie grabbed her jacket and put her open bag on the bed. 'Could you jump inside again? Just to be on the safe side. I'm going to find Dad.'

Mr Allen was in the garage, tidying his tool kit. He looked up and smiled as Sadie came in. 'I expect you want your pocket money.'

'Yes, please,' Sadie said.

She nearly died on the spot when Flame popped his head up out of the bag. Then she remembered that her dad couldn't see him.

'Here you are, love . . .' Mr Allen's eyes started watering. He gave a big sniff. 'That's funny. I must be getting a cold. Ah-choo!'

'Poor you,' Sadie said hurrying
outside. 'Thanks for the money, Dad.
See you later.'

'Right you are,' her dad answered.
'Ah-choo!'

Sadie and Flame reached the shops,
but Jenny wasn't there yet. Sadie sat on
a bench to wait for her. She glanced
around and then whispered to Flame.
'It's OK for you to show yourself. I
can't see any neighbours or anyone
who knows me.'

Flame jumped into her lap and
settled down. As Sadie stroked him,
watching people going in and out of
the shops, a shaggy little dog, trailing a
lead behind it, ran up to her. She
recognized him straightaway.

'Presto!' Sadie reached out and caught
hold of his lead. 'Where's Lena? Have
you run off, you naughty dog?'

Presto gave her a doggy grin.
Wagging his tail, he woofed softly at
Flame. Flame's whiskers twitched. He
began purring and then jumped down
beside the little dog.

'How sweet. They're making friends!'

Sadie looked up, surprised to see
Lena looking down at Flame and
Presto. 'Hi, Lena!'

'Hi, Sadie. I'm glad you were here!'

Lena replied. 'Presto jerked the lead out of my hand and took off! Thanks for holding on to the little rascal.'

At that moment Jenny arrived too. 'Sorry I'm late,' she said breathlessly, reaching the two girls. Her face fell when she saw Lena. 'Oh. Hello.'

Lena smiled at Jenny. 'Hi. I love your new haircut. It's really nice.'

Jenny didn't reply but then spotted Flame for the first time. Her eyes widened. 'Where did you get that cute kitten, Lena? Is it yours?'

Sadie shook her head. 'He's mine. He's called Flame. I found him last night – I'm looking after him.'

Lena leaned down to stroke Flame. 'He's gorgeous, Sadie.'

'Yeah, definitely,' agreed Jenny. 'I like his

name. But how come your dad let you have him? He's allergic to cats, isn't he?'

'Dad doesn't know about Flame,' Sadie admitted. 'I'm hiding him in my bedroom for now. You have to promise that you won't say anything to my parents.' Sadie felt a little bad at not telling Jenny the whole truth but she decided that she probably wouldn't have believed her anyway!

'Cool! A secret kitten. OK. I promise,' Jenny said. 'But I wouldn't like to be you, when your dad finds out!'

Sadie rolled her eyes. 'I'll worry about that when it happens.'

Lena chuckled. 'I'm just about to go back home to the circus school. I wondered if you'd both like to come back for some tea, and meet my mum and dad and the rest of our troupe,' she said.

Delighted at the idea, Sadie jumped at the chance. 'Thanks very much. We'd love to, wouldn't we, Jenny?'

'Oh, I was going to suggest that we went to the cinema,' Jenny said quietly.

'We can do that any time!' Sadie said.

Jenny hesitated for a second then she smiled. 'I suppose we can. Tea sounds great, Lena.'

The circus was only a few minutes' walk away. It had once been a cinema and now was painted in cheerful red and yellow stripes to look like a big top. There were bright-blue pillars dotted with silver stars either side of the main door.

Colourful posters announced the
dates and times of the performances.

'I've always wondered what it's like
inside here,' Sadie whispered to Flame.
She held him in her arms and he
looked round curiously as they went
through a gate into a huge yard. Men
and women in leotards and track pants
leapt and tumbled on circus equipment
in front of them as they followed Lena
to a modern trailer.

Inside the trailer smelt of lemon
polish. There was a big sofa and chairs
with lots of bright cushions. Sparkling
glass and china ornaments lined the
window sills.

'Mum, Dad, I've brought someone to
meet you,' Lena said. She turned to
Jenny and Sadie. 'These are my parents.
Olga and Victor Tomani.'

Sadie smiled at Lena's parents, who
both had olive skin and dark hair.
Victor Tomani bore a strong
resemblance to his daughter. 'Hi, I'm
Sadie. Nice to meet you,' she said.

'Me too. I'm Jenny,' Jenny said.

'It's so nice to meet some of Lena's
friends,' said Olga Tomani with a warm
smile. 'Do sit down.'

Olga made tea and set out plates of

sandwiches and cakes. There was even a dish of sardines for Flame and a meaty bone for Presto.

Flame gave a purr of delight and began chomping the sardines.

Victor glanced at him. 'A black cat is lucky, especially with such bright-green eyes. This little one is very special,' he said softly to Sadie.

Sadie smiled. He didn't have to tell her that!

As she and Jenny nibbled slices of delicious chocolate cake, Olga brought out a scrapbook. Sadie and Jenny enjoyed leafing through, looking at cuttings with pictures of Lena in circus rings all over the world. She had been performing since she was four years old.

'You might say that sawdust is in my blood!' Lena said proudly.

'Sounds uncomfortable!' Jenny exclaimed, as everyone laughed.

Flame and Presto had finished eating and were curled up together on the sofa. When it was time to leave, Sadie had to tickle Flame under the chin to wake him up.

'You will come again, won't you?' Lena asked as the girls were about to leave.

'We'd love to, thanks a lot!' Sadie said eagerly.

She expected Jenny to say the same, but her friend remained unusually silent as they left the trailer.

Sadie, Jenny and Flame retraced their steps across the yard. The acrobats were

still practising. There was a sheen of
sweat on their bodies. Sadie felt like she
could have watched them forever.

As they walked back home, Sadie was
relieved that Jenny seemed to have
cheered up. She had noticed how quiet
she had been at Lena's. She thought
about what she might get Jenny for her
birthday in a few days.

'I just need to pop to the shops,'
Sadie told her. 'Why don't you go on
without me?'

'OK. I'll see you on Monday,' Jenny
said.

'I'll call for you before school. And
don't forget we're going to circus youth
club afterwards!' Sadie reminded her.

'As if you'd let me forget! See you!'
Jenny walked away.

After buying Flame's cat food, Sadie
realized that she didn't have much
money for Jenny's present. She
wandered around the shelves, looking
for something she could afford.

Flame poked his head out of her bag
and watched Sadie pick up a big
notebook with sequins and beads on
the cover.

'Oh, that's gorgeous.' Sadie looked at

the notebook for a moment and then put it back reluctantly.

Flame frowned. 'Is something wrong?'

'No. It's just that Jenny would have loved that book.' She picked up a smaller plain notebook and a purple pen, with a pink heart that lit up when you used it. 'This book's not as nice. But it's all I can afford. I hope Jenny won't mind.'

As she went to pay for the notebook and pen, Sadie didn't see the thoughtful look on Flame's face.

When Sadie reached home, she opened the front door carefully. She could hear her parents talking in the kitchen. Creeping upstairs, she hid the tins of cat food in the bottom of her wardrobe and put the plastic carrier with Jenny's present inside on her bed.

Flame jumped up and curled up on the duvet. He yawned, showing his little sharp teeth.

'I expect you're ready for a nap after those sardines. I'll see you later.' Sadie patted him and went downstairs to the kitchen.

Her mum was reading the paper, while her dad boiled the kettle for hot chocolate.

'Hello, love. I didn't hear you come in,' Mr Allen said. 'Did you and Jenny have a good time?'

'The best! You'll never guess where we've been.' Sadie slipped into a chair next to her mum. She told them about meeting Lena's parents. 'We had sandwiches and cake. And there were even sardines for . . .' she broke off. She had just been about to mention Flame! '. . . for me,' she said hurriedly.

Her mum frowned. 'You hate sardines!'

'I don't any more. I love them, yum yum,' Sadie fibbed madly. 'Anyway,' she rushed on. 'We looked through this amazing scrapbook with cuttings and –'

Suddenly there was the most enormous thud from upstairs.

Sadie froze.

Her dad stopped in the middle of stirring hot water into chocolate powder. 'What was that?'

'Er . . . What? I didn't hear anything,' Sadie said, her heart thumping.

Her dad eyed her suspiciously. 'That

noise. It came from your bedroom. I'd better go and have a look.'

'No!' Sadie burst out. What if Flame was asleep and didn't have time to make himself invisible? 'I mean, I'll go first!'

'Sadie?' Mr Allen called after his daughter as she shot out of the kitchen.

Sadie felt an unusual warm tingling down her spine as she hurtled up the stairs two at a time. She didn't have time to think about it – her dad was right behind her. Yanking open the bedroom door, she almost threw herself inside, and then leaned against it to hold it shut.

'Oh, no!' she gasped. How on earth was she going to explain this?

Chapter
* FOUR *

Flame stood on the bed, his black
coat fizzing with silver sparks and
his whiskers crackling with
electricity.

The plastic bag with Jenny's
notebook inside lay on the floor, where
it had fallen. Sadie gasped. No wonder
it had made such a noise. The bag was
now as big as a bedside rug! Starbursts

of coloured glitter sprayed out of it in all directions.

There was no time for explanations.

'Dad's coming! Do something!' she hissed at Flame.

Flame looked a little hurt, but waved his paw towards the enormous bag.

Instantly the bag shrank and the sprays of coloured glitter whizzed back towards Flame's paw.

'Sadie?' Her dad banged on her

bedroom door. 'Open up! Why are you holding this door shut?'

'Flame!' Sadie exclaimed.

Flame vanished. There was only a tiny dent in the quilt where his invisible little form lay.

'Just give me a minute!' Sadie sang out. She thought quickly. Dashing over to a cupboard, she dragged out an armful of clothes and scattered them on the floor.

The door banged open and her dad stepped inside. 'What's going on in here?' he demanded.

Sadie turned round and looked at him innocently. 'What? Oh, you mean that noise? The bag with Jenny's present inside slid on to the floor.'

Her dad glanced at it. 'It made a very

loud noise for such a small bag. Why did you hold the door closed?'

'I was . . . er . . . trying to put this stuff away. I didn't want you to see how messy my room was.' Sadie jammed a T-shirt back into the cupboard.

Mr Allen rubbed his nose. His eyes started to water. 'Ah–choo!' he sneezed.

'It must be all the dust in here,' Sadie said quickly, starting to edge him out of the room. 'I'll get the hoover.'

Mr Allen's eyes almost popped out of his head. 'Hoover? Ah–choo! Are you sure you're feeling OK?'

'I'm fine. I'm great. Hoovering is no big deal, you know!' Sadie gabbled, standing in the doorway. She watched until she was certain he had gone, before she went back in and collapsed on to the bed. 'Phew! That was much too close.'

Flame padded across the bed and rubbed his head apologetically against Sadie's arm. 'I was trying to make Jenny's present more special. But I used too much magic and it grew extra big!' he mewed softly.

Sadie couldn't help laughing. 'You can say that again! Never mind. Everything's back to normal now.'

Flame looked surprised. 'You are not angry?'

Sadie stroked his soft little ears. 'I could never be angry with you. You were only trying to help.'

She bent down to pick up the carrier bag and then looked inside. 'Oh!' she gasped. The small plain notebook had

gone. In its place was a larger version
in pink velvet and decorated with shiny
beads and purple thread. 'It's gorgeous!
It even matches the pen. Jenny's going
to adore this. Thanks ever so much,
Flame!'

'I really want to work in the circus
when I'm old enough,' Sadie confided
to Jenny as they left school that day for
the circus youth group.

Flame's head poked out of Sadie's
bag, taking in everything with his big
emerald eyes.

'Working in the circus?' Jenny said,
giggling. 'What are you going to call
yourself? The Flying Sadie? More like
the Flopping-about Sadie, I should
think!' She galloped down the path,

waving her arms up and down. 'Look at me, I'm a famous trapeze artist!' she said in a snooty voice before collapsing in fits of laughter.

Sadie couldn't help but laugh. Jenny did look hilarious prancing about like that. But she wished she hadn't said anything now.

'I don't mean I want to work in the circus now!' she said when Jenny had stopped laughing. 'That *would* be stupid. I know I'd have to work really hard to get anywhere near good enough. But if Lena can do it, so can I. Everyone has to start somewhere, don't they?'

'Can't we talk about something else for a change?' Jenny grumbled.

Sadie stared at her friend in surprise, taken aback. She gave Jenny a sheepish grin. 'Sorry. I suppose I have been going on a bit, haven't I? Just tell me to shut up if I go on circus overload.'

Sadie felt a bit nervous as they reached the circus youth club. Lots of kids had turned up and the place was crowded.

'Come on, Flame. Let's find somewhere to get changed,' Sadie said, walking across the room with Flame in her arms.

'Fancy talking to a kitten. As if it's going to answer her!' a voice jeered.

It was Grace Davies, a loud girl who was always messing about in class.

Sadie felt herself going red. 'Why are you bothered? I wasn't talking to you!' she said.

Grace flushed but remained silent. Someone tittered. Sadie saw Jenny trying not to laugh as she stood up.

'Let's go and get changed.' Jenny linked arms with Sadie. 'Sorry I was moody earlier.'

'That's OK. I'm really glad you're here,' Sadie said as they strolled across the room together.

'Really?' Jenny looked uncertain.

'You're my best friend, aren't you?'

Sadie said happily. 'It wouldn't be half as much fun without you.'

'Hi, Sadie! Hi, Jenny!' Lena called as the girls returned from getting changed. Presto was at her heels. 'Oh, good, you've brought Flame with you. I was hoping you would.'

As Sadie put Flame down, Presto gave an eager little yap. Flame purred loudly and Presto wagged his tail as they sniffed each other.

Victor Tomani clapped his hands to get everyone's attention. 'Welcome! Would you all gather round? I want a quick word about the aims of the youth club and then we'll move on to doing some warm-ups.'

'I think I might faint with

excitement,' Grace boomed, patting her mouth and faking a yawn.

Jenny chuckled. 'Grace's a riot, isn't she?'

'No!' Sadie said, annoyed. 'I don't know why she bothered to come.'

'She doesn't mean anything,' Jenny said.

'If you ask me, she's a real pain. I came here to learn stuff, not listen to her foghorn voice!' Sadie grumbled.

Jenny looked at her. 'I thought we came to have fun,' she said quietly.

Sadie didn't answer. She was listening to what Victor was saying about learning circus skills helping with kids' self-confidence.

'OK, lecture over!' he said after a few more minutes. 'We have plenty of helpers to assist you. Make sure you ask someone if you are unsure about anything. There are lots of skills to try. I suggest you divide into groups and see how you get on.'

Sadie joined a group being taught by Lena and her mum. 'See you later. Have fun!' she waved as Jenny passed by on her way over to an area with baskets holding clubs, hoops and soft foam balls.

'Have any of you used a springboard?' Olga asked.

Sadie and three other girls raised their hands.

'OK, you four come over here with Lena,' Olga said. 'I'll work with the rest of you on the mats.'

As Sadie waited for her turn, she glanced over at Jenny and was amazed to see her juggling three balls. Jenny saw her and grinned delightedly. Sadie waved. She was so happy that Jenny was enjoying herself.

'Off you go, Sadie,' Lena prompted.

Sadie turned back to the springboard. She took a deep breath and ran forward. Just as she bounced on to the springboard, Grace's loud complaining voice floated into the air.

'This is a waste of time! It's boring,
boring, boring! Can't I do something
else?'

Sadie's concentration wobbled. As she
rose into the air she felt herself twisting
awkwardly. She was going to fall!

Chapter
FIVE

Panic flashed through Sadie's mind.
As she tensed for a painful and
embarrassing landing, she saw Flame
scampering towards her.

He raised a paw and Sadie felt a
warm tingling feeling in her spine.
Suddenly a snowstorm of bright glittery
sparks surrounded Sadie and she
whooshed higher and higher into the

air. She flipped over and over into a backspin and then did a half-twist before landing perfectly with her arms outstretched.

A burst of riotous applause rang out.

Sadie stood there, stunned. She couldn't believe she was unhurt. Flame had saved her!

'Well done, Sadie,' Lena praised. 'That was amazing!'

Sadie looked at Flame, who winked. No one else appeared to have seen the magical sparks around her, and those in Flame's fur had now faded.

Sadie blushed like mad. 'It was a fluke. I could never do it again,' she said modestly. *Not without Flame's help*, she thought to herself.

Olga put her hand on Sadie's

shoulder. 'Don't set limits for yourself. We're all capable of more than we realize, especially you it seems!'

Sadie nodded. 'Thanks for the advice.'

She still felt a bit shaky as she went and sat down. Flame bounded over and jumped into her lap. 'Are you all right, Sadie?' he purred softly.

'Yes. Thanks to you. You're brilliant, Flame. You saved me from really hurting myself,' she replied in a whisper.

Flame blinked at her with bright emerald eyes. 'You are welcome.'

At the end of youth club, Sadie pulled on her tracksuit and said goodbye to Lena. Flame trotted along happily at her feet as she followed Jenny outside. 'I saw you juggling those balls. You're really good.'

'As if you're bothered,' Jenny
murmured.

Sadie swung round, stung. 'What do
you mean?'

Jenny's face was tight and set. 'You
just can't help showing off in front of
Lena and everyone, can you?'

'But I didn't. I almost fell and . . .'
Sadie stopped. She could hardly tell
Jenny that Flame had used his magic to
save her.

Grace and some other girls from their school walked past. 'Are you coming?' Grace called to Jenny.

Jenny nodded and turned her back on Sadie. 'I'm not walking home with you. I promised to go over Grace's history homework with her,' she shouted without looking round.

Sadie stared after her friend in surprise. Since when had Jenny been helping anyone with their homework?

Flame whined softly to be picked up. Sadie held him gently.

He touched her chin with the tip of his cold nose. 'I have made everything worse between you and Jenny. I am sorry,' he mewed sadly.

Sadie kissed the top of his tiny head. 'It's not your fault. It's mine. Somehow,

I keep upsetting Jenny and I don't know how to make things right between us.'

A couple of days later it was Jenny's birthday. Sadie decided to post the present and card through Jenny's letter box before school that morning. She didn't quite feel brave enough to give them to her at school.

'I couldn't bear it if she threw them back at me,' Sadie told Flame.

Flame wrinkled his furry little brow. 'I do not think Jenny is that kind of person.'

Sadie didn't think so either, but she wasn't taking any risks. As Sadie went to deliver the present, Jenny's mum opened the door.

'Hello, Mrs Coleman,' Sadie said politely. 'Will you give Jenny this, please?'

'Hello, Sadie. Why don't you come in and give it to her yourself? It might cheer her up. She's not feeling very well.'

'What's the matter with her? Isn't she coming to school?' Sadie asked.

Mrs Coleman shook her head. 'Not today. She's got a tummy ache. I'm sure it's not serious. Are you coming in to say hello?'

Sadie hesitated. A familiar loud laugh floated out of the door. Grace was already with Jenny. 'No. Just tell her I called. I hope she feels better soon.'

The school day dragged for Sadie. Despite their last argument, she really missed her best friend. She hoped Grace Davies hadn't taken her place.

Back at home in her room, she was

feeding Flame when her mum called up the stairs, 'Sadie! Jenny's on the phone!'

Sadie dashed downstairs two at a time and grabbed the phone. 'Thanks, Mum. Hi, Jenny! Are you feeling better?'

'Yes. I'm fine now. Thanks for my birthday present. I love the notebook. It was nice of you to remember.' Jenny's voice was polite but distant.

'Course I remembered!' Sadie said. How could Jenny think she would forget her birthday?

'Why didn't you come in and cheer me up?' Jenny asked. 'You knew I was feeling rotten.'

'I would have. But that noise-monster Grace Davies was already in there with you. Anyone a hundred miles away could hear her cheering you up!' she joked.

Jenny didn't laugh. 'Grace's OK when you get to know her.'

Sadie didn't want to get to know Grace better. She just wanted things back as they were between her and Jenny. 'Are you coming back to school tomorrow?'

'Yes. Look, I've got to go now. Bye.'
Jenny rang off.

Sadie dragged her feet as she went
back upstairs. Jenny had probably only
phoned out of politeness. She lay on
her bed with Flame beside her. As she
stroked him his whole body vibrated
with his purring.

'I'm glad I've got you for my friend,'
Sadie said, feeling comforted. 'I don't
know what I'd do without you.'

Chapter
* SIX *

Over the next week, Sadie saw Jenny at
school and at youth club, but she never
got the chance to talk to her alone.
Jenny was always with Grace and some
other girls.

'Have you and Jenny fallen out?'
Lena asked one evening as Sadie helped
put away the exercise mats.

'She's got a new best friend. She

doesn't need me any more,' Sadie said, trying to sound as if she didn't care. To her horror she felt her eyes filling with tears.

Lena looked sympathetic. She put her arm round Sadie's shoulders. 'Give her some time. Maybe she'll come round.'

'Maybe,' Sadie agreed, wiping her eyes.

'I've got something for you.' Lena gave Sadie a handful of tickets.

'Wow! Ringside seats for the circus!'

Lena nodded. 'It's our first performance of the season this Saturday. Everyone from the youth club is invited. Bring your mum and dad too. Do you think you'll be able to come?'

Sadie gave her a watery smile. This was just what she needed to cheer her up. 'Try and stop me!'

'I'll take my shoulder bag. If I put it on my lap with the zip open you can watch the performance,' Sadie said to Flame on Saturday evening.

Flame nodded. 'I would like that very much.'

Sadie ran down to where her parents were waiting in the car on the drive.

'Do you really need to take that huge bag?' her dad asked.

'Yes,' Sadie said firmly. 'It's got stuff inside that I need.' She hoped he wouldn't ask what. 'Come on, Dad. We'll be late!'

'All right! Hold your horses.' Her dad smiled as he started the car and pulled out on to the road.

Sadie could feel herself getting more and more excited as they went into the circus school building. She settled herself in her ringside seat next to her parents, with her bag on her knees. Jenny came in with her parents and, to Sadie's surprise, sat in the empty seat next to her.

Sadie wondered if Lena had something to do with it.

'Hi,' she said to Jenny, with a nervous smile. 'This should be good.'

Jenny nodded. 'Yes,' she said shortly.

Sadie's heart leapt with hope. At least Jenny wasn't ignoring her.

The circus ring was ablaze with colour and flashing lights. A burst of music rang out and the ring-mistress, in a top hat and tails and shiny boots, stepped through a star-covered curtain into the ring. 'Ladies and gentlemen.

Boys and girls! Welcome to Bullard's Circus!'

Jugglers on stilts and unicycles, tumblers and acrobats, a human pyramid and a dozen more acts all performed in a riot of sound and colour.

Flame seemed to be enjoying it too. Sadie saw his wide emerald eyes peeking out from her bag as he took everything in.

Next came the clowns. 'We need the help of someone from the audience,' shouted a clown with a white face, a red nose and fuzzy blue hair. 'You? Yes, you! Would you come here, please?' he asked, pointing to Jenny.

Jenny went bright pink. She tried to shrink back into her seat, but willing hands pushed her forward. The clowns gathered around whispering instructions. Jenny was given a red wig and helped into a pair of baggy checked dungarees.

Sadie watched in amazement as Jenny juggled six soft balls. She was really good.

Then Jenny dropped a ball.

Sadie's heart missed a beat. But Jenny didn't seem to care. She put a finger to her mouth and pulled a mournful face. The crowd howled with laughter.

'They think it's part of the act,' Sadie whispered to Flame. 'Jenny's a natural, isn't she?'

Then came the act Sadie had been waiting for.

The Flying Tomanis made daring

leaps, turns and catches on the trapeze high up above a safety net. The women wore exotic make-up and tiaras that twinkled in the lights. Sadie hardly recognized Olga, Victor and Lena. They looked so glamorous and mysterious. Lena hung from a trapeze by the tips of her toes and Sadie gasped with delight and fear.

When the show ended all the performers took a bow – including Jenny – and Sadie applauded until her palms ached.

As her parents filed out after the performance, Sadie hung back. 'That was amazing,' she whispered to Flame. 'Wasn't it clever of Lena to arrange for the clowns to single Jenny out?' She sighed. 'I hope I'll be good enough to work in the circus one day.'

'You will be very good indeed, Sadie,' Flame mewed confidently. 'You must follow your dream.'

Sadie stroked him gently. Flame wasn't only special because he was magic; he was also the best kind of friend. The sort that made you feel stronger and better about yourself.

Outside the circus, Sadie saw Jenny and her parents. On impulse, she ran up to her friend. 'You were fantastic. And you didn't seem at all nervous in the ring. Everyone loved it.'

'Thanks.' Jenny smiled hesitantly. 'Um . . . I'd better go. Mum and Dad are waiting in the car for me.'

When Jenny and her parents passed by in their car, Jenny waved. Sadie felt

her heart swell and was sure that they
would soon make up properly.

Sadie rejoined her mum and dad just
as a little door in the side of the circus
opened. Lena popped her head out. She
was still wearing her stage make-up.
'Hi, Sadie! Did you enjoy the show?'
she called.

'It was wonderful! Fantastic!' Sadie
enthused.

Presto shot out from behind Lena
and made a beeline for Sadie's shoulder
bag. Jumping up and down, he whined
excitedly for Flame to come out and
play.

'Uh-oh,' Sadie murmured, gently
pushing the little dog away from her
bag with one foot. 'Shoo! Go away,
Presto!'

Any minute now her parents were
going to wonder what was going on.

Presto put his front paws on Sadie's
bag and scrabbled, trying to nose his
way inside.

'What's he after?' her dad wanted to
know.

Sadie's heart sank, but she put on her
most innocent expression. 'No, er, idea.'

'Hmm.' Mr Allen bent down. He
started to undo the bag's zipper.

It's going to be OK. Flame's invisible,
Sadie comforted herself silently.

And then everything happened at
once.

A large brown and white dog shot
out of a nearby alleyway. It spotted
Presto and came bounding towards
him. Presto yelped with terror. He
dived head first into Sadie's half-open
shoulder bag and landed on Flame.

'Yeo-row-row!' Flame screeched with
surprise.

'What the . . .' Mr Allen gasped.

Sadie made a frantic grab for her bag,
but the big dog beat her to it. It
grasped it in its enormous teeth and
began dragging it towards the alleyway.

'Hey! Come back!' Sadie yelled.

She dashed into the dark alleyway,

followed closely by her parents. There
was no time to think of a plan. She
had to get the bag away from the dog
somehow. Flame wouldn't risk using his
magic with her mum and dad so close.

The dog had backed up against a
wall. It had dropped the bag, but stood
over it, growling menacingly. Sadie
daren't risk trying to grab the bag
while it was within reach of those huge
sharp teeth.

She suddenly remembered that she
had a half-eaten tube of aniseed sweets
in her pocket. Dogs loved the smell of
aniseed, didn't they? Taking out the
sweets, she waved them about. The dog
sniffed the air and licked its chops.

Hoping like mad that she could
distract the dog for even a few seconds,

Sadie rolled two sweets down the
alley. The dog crept forward, keeping a
wary eye on her, before darting
towards the sweets and crunching
them up.

Quick as a flash, her heart beating
fast, Sadie lurched forward and seized
the bag. She threw the rest of the tube
of sweets at the dog and hurtled out of
the alley.

As soon as she was safely in the street outside, Sadie opened her bag. 'Are you all right, Flame?' she panted. 'I thought that horrible dog was going to eat you!' As she picked him up, a few sparks in his black fur fizzed against her hand before they went out.

Flame rubbed his head against her arm. 'I am fine. Thank you for saving me, Sadie. You were very brave. You could have been badly bitten,' he purred.

'I just couldn't bear to let him hurt you,' Sadie said, trying to catch her breath. Now that she thought about the danger she had been in, her knees felt all weak and wobbly.

Sadie reached into her bag with her free hand and lifted Presto out. The little dog was trembling from head to foot. He gave a relieved little yap and began licking Flame's ears.

'Sadie?'

Mr and Mrs Allen stared at the little dog and the fluffy black kitten in their daughter's arms and then looked down at the open shoulder bag.

Sadie looked at her parents. Flame hadn't had time to make himself invisible. *I'm in so much trouble*, she thought.

'Is there something you want to tell me, young lady?' her dad said sternly.

Chapter
★ SEVEN ★

Sadie realized there was only one
possible thing to do. She burst into tears.

'Oh, dear!' Mrs Allen rushed up and
put her arm round Sadie's shoulders.
'You're all shaken up, love! Did that big
dog bite you?'

Sadie shook her head. 'I'm fine. It's
not that. It's . . . it's . . . everything,' she
sobbed.

Her mum gave her a cuddle. 'I knew
it. You and Jenny haven't been getting
on like you used to, have you?'

Mr Allen stared at his wife and
daughter in confusion. 'What's that got
to do with that kitten?' he asked,
mystified. 'No wonder I've been
sneezing! Sadie's had that little mite in
the house. In her bedroom too, I
shouldn't wonder.'

'We'll get to that in a minute,' his

wife answered calmly, passing Sadie a tissue. 'Can't you see that Sadie's upset?'

Sadie gulped and wept, realizing for the first time that she was actually crying for real. She couldn't stop. It had all been so mixed up between her and Jenny lately. Having Flame as a friend had helped her cope. Now it looked as if she might lose him too and she didn't think she could bear it.

'About this kitten . . .' Mr Allen tried again.

Sadie gave a loud wail. 'I can't give up Flame! He's my f . . . friend.' She looked at her dad through her tears. 'Please, please, please let me keep him,' she begged

Mr Allen looked at his wife who nodded slowly. 'Well – if he's that important to you, I suppose he can stay,' he decided. 'But you must make sure he stays in your bedroom.'

'I will!' Sadie almost threw herself into her dad's arms and then she remembered she was holding Flame. 'I'll make sure I keep Flame miles away from you. And I'll buy you a giant box of tissues, just in case! Thanks, Dad. You're the best!'

Back at youth club on Monday, everyone was talking about the circus performance. Victor Tomani smiled at all the eager faces. 'I'm glad you found it inspiring. Because you're all going to get a chance to perform!'

'What do you think he means?' Sadie said to Jenny, who was standing next to her. At least they were speaking again now, although Jenny had arrived with Grace.

Jenny shrugged. 'I don't know.'

'There's a carnival in a couple of weeks' time,' Victor continued. 'And I've been asked if the youth club would like to take part. We're putting up a circus ring in the park, where the carnival ends up. So you can put on a display.'

Everyone started talking at once.

'OK, details can come later,' said Victor, shouting above the noise. 'You need to decide what you want to do. I suggest you team up in twos and threes and work out some routines.'

Sadie didn't have to think about it. There was only one person she wanted to team up with.

'Come on, Flame,' she said. With him at her heel, she turned round to Jenny before she lost her nerve.

Jenny had her back to Sadie and turned round in surprise as Sadie shook her arm.

'Why don't you and I get together?' Sadie said excitedly. 'We could be a comedy double act with acrobatics and juggling. I don't mind wearing a clown suit . . .'

'Look at her trailing around with the kitten! She's trying to be just like Lena with Presto!' Grace scoffed.

'Oh, shut up, Grace!' Sadie snapped impatiently. 'What do you think, Jenny?'

'I don't know . . .' Jenny looked uncertain.

'Well, I do!' Grace planted herself in

front of Jenny. 'You've hardly bothered
with her for ages. Now you're sucking
up, just because Lena's too busy
rehearsing to make a fuss of you!'

Sadie's jaw dropped. 'That's rubbish.
Jenny? You don't believe that, do you?'

Jenny flushed. 'I don't want to. But
Grace does have a point . . .'

Sadie felt a hot wave of anger. This
was so unfair. She stamped away, her
fists bunching with temper. 'Fine!' she
shouted over her shoulder. 'Believe
what you like! I wouldn't team up with
you now, Jenny Coleman — even if you
paid me!'

That night, Sadie lay awake staring into
the dark for ages. She wished she could
take back what she'd said to Jenny. It

had only made things a hundred times worse and now she didn't know how to make them better.

She sighed. It was no good, she couldn't get to sleep. Sadie switched on her bedside lamp and shook Flame gently.

'Flame? Are you asleep?' she whispered.

He sat up and shook himself. 'Is something wrong, Sadie?' he miaowed softly.

'I can't stop thinking about Jenny. How can I make her believe that I really want to work with her?'

Suddenly she thought of something. 'I know what to do! But I'm going to need lots of help. Listen, Flame . . .'

Flame pricked up his ears as Sadie
outlined her plan. 'When shall we do
this?' he asked solemnly.

'Right now! There won't be anyone
about.' Sadie slipped out of bed and
started getting dressed. 'We'll have to be
really quiet. If Mum and Dad discover
that I've gone out in the middle of the
night, I'll be grounded for a year.'

Sadie quickly grabbed a spare sheet
from the airing cupboard and rolled it

up. She crept downstairs with
Flame and went outside. The street
was very quiet and a bit spooky with
only the light from the few street
lamps.

Sadie shivered. She was really glad
that Flame was with her.

With Flame bounding beside her,
Sadie jogged the short distance to the
circus. 'We need somewhere where we
won't be seen if any cars pass by. Let's
go into the alleyway where that big
dog came from.'

Flame mewed in agreement.

In the alleyway, Sadie shook out the
sheet and laid it on the ground. 'OK. It
needs to be big and colourful if we
want everyone to notice it.'

'That is no problem!' Flame's fluffy

black fur began fizzing all over with bright sparks.

Sadie felt a familiar tingling sensation down her spine as Flame raised a tiny paw. A shower of glitter shot into the air and then trickled down on to the sheet. The sheet rippled and began to grow bigger and bigger until it was a huge oblong shape.

Flame's face crinkled in concentration and then suddenly — splatter! Bright-blue and yellow dye slashed across the white cotton from out of nowhere. Whoosh! Fringed gold braid snaked around the edges. Crackle! Big red sequins popped down one by one, making big, fancy letters spread across the full length of the sheet.

'Wow! That's fantastic — even better

than I'd imagined. Thank you so much, Flame!'

'I am glad you are pleased,' Flame mewed proudly.

'Now we have to fix it to the wall somehow,' Sadie said.

'Leave this to me.' Flame sent another glowing cloud of sparks into the air.

The sparks divided up and formed four shapes like glittery hands. Sadie watched in amazement as the magic hands each grabbed a corner of the banner and rose into the night air.

She and Flame ran out of the alleyway. The banner floated towards the circus, where the hands placed it against the wall. It hung there as if held in place by superglue. Their job done, the sparkly hands dissolved and

showered down on Sadie and
Flame.

Sadie looked up at the banner as the
sparkles rained down around her. 'Well,
if that doesn't bring Jenny round,
nothing will! Thanks for helping me,'
she said to Flame, stifling a yawn. 'I
think I'll be able to sleep now. I just
hope we can creep back into the house
without anyone seeing us.'

Flame grinned and once more his whiskers crackled. There was a bright-blue flash.

Sadie felt something soft and cool against her cheek. She pushed herself away and stared – it was her pillow! She was in her own bed. The duvet dipped as Flame jumped up and settled down beside her. In no time at all, Sadie fell into a deep sleep.

Chapter
* EIGHT *

High up on the circus wall the huge
banner fluttered, with the evening sun
twinkling on its shiny braid and
glittering red letters. It read:

'The Amazing Jenny and Sadie.
Come and see this brand-new act at
the carnival.'

As Sadie and Flame turned the
corner, they almost bumped into a

small crowd of kids staring up at it.
Sadie saw that Jenny and Grace were in
the middle of them. Jenny spotted
Sadie and broke away from the group.

'She's coming over! I hope this
works,' Sadie whispered nervously to
Flame.

'Hi,' Jenny said awkwardly.

'Hi,' Sadie replied. 'Um . . . What do
you think of the banner?'

'It's pretty amazing. How did you get
it up there?'

'I had some help,' Sadie said vaguely.
'Look, I'm sorry about losing my
temper the other day. Please believe I
always wanted to be your partner.'

'I do,' Jenny said. She bit her lip. 'I
don't believe everything Grace tells me,
you know. She was just looking out for

me. She knows how much I hate it when you and I argue.'

'Does she?' Grace went slightly up in Sadie's opinion. Maybe she wasn't so bad, after all. She gave Jenny a sheepish grin. 'It looks like I've been a bit of an idiot.'

'We both have,' Jenny said. She gave Sadie a hug. 'Best friends again?'

'You bet!' Sadie returned the hug. 'So, what do you think of our name?'

Jenny beamed at her. 'I love it. The Amazing Jenny and Sadie! We're going to be a riot – let's go into the youth club and start work now!'

By the end of the session, Sadie and Jenny had worked out their act. They decided to keep it simple. Sadie was going to walk on her hands and do some tumbling, while Jenny walked beside her, juggling.

They'd put in extra practice over the weekend and in any spare moments at school. Lena had offered to lend them costumes, so everything was looking good.

'Have you seen Flame?' Sadie said to Jenny as they got ready to go home. She suddenly realized that she hadn't seen him for a while.

Jenny shook her head. 'He was here a minute ago.'

Flame had never gone off by himself before. Warning bells went off in Sadie's mind.

She went off to search for him. She finally found Flame cowering behind a pile of exercise mats. 'Flame? What's wrong?' she whispered, picking him up.

Flame's entire body was trembling and his emerald eyes glittered with terror. 'I can sense my uncle's spies. They are getting close,' he whined softly.

'Oh, no!' Sadie went cold all over. She had hoped that this day would never come. 'I . . . I guess that means you have to leave.'

She held Flame close. She could feel his tiny heart beating fast against her hand. Although she tried to stay calm, a lump rose in Sadie's throat. She wasn't ready to let Flame go yet.

Suddenly he pricked up his ears and she felt him start to relax. Flame gave a gruff little mew of relief. 'My enemies are moving away. The danger is over – for now.'

'Thank goodness,' Sadie breathed. 'I was really scared. So – you'll stay here, with me?'

Flame nodded. 'For a little longer. If they return I must leave. Maybe without warning.'

'I understand,' Sadie said softly as she put him inside her bag. His enemies hadn't found him this time. But they would keep looking, and both she and Flame knew that they wouldn't give up.

Flame sat on a cupboard in Sadie's bedroom, watching Sadie and Jenny finish practising their act. His emerald eyes were creased in contentment.

'That wasn't bad. Even if I say so myself!' Jenny said, as she packed her things away after their session.

'Good, because the carnival's tomorrow,' Sadie said.

Jenny pulled a face. 'Pretty scary. But it's exciting too!'

Sadie nodded. 'I can't wait. Just think, we're going to be part of the parade with *real* circus acts!'

She went downstairs with Jenny to say goodbye.

Flame turned to look at her as she came back to her room. 'I am glad that you and Jenny are friends again,' he purred happily.

'Me too.' Sadie ran his silky black tail through her hand. 'I can't even remember why we fell out. And I'm *really* glad I don't have to hide you from Mum and Dad any more. Dad's not even sneezing as much when he's near you. You could live here with me

forever, you know, if you wanted to.'

Flame blinked slowly, a gentle look on his tiny fluffy face. 'That is not possible, Sadie.'

Sadie sighed and gave him a cuddle. 'I know. But I'm trying hard not to think about that.'

The rousing sound of the brass band filled the air. A drum major marched along, twirling his baton as he led the carnival parade. Decorated lorries and floats came next.

Behind them, led by the ring-mistress in a black top hat and shiny black boots, came the circus performers.

The Flying Tomanis were on a float decorated with silver balloons and sparkling bunting. It even had a trapeze and they took turns to perform as the lorry trundled along the street. Presto sat beside Lena, wearing a tiny silver coat and wagging his tail madly.

Sadie and Jenny walked alongside the Tomanis' float. One of the clowns had lent Jenny a costume. She looked amazing in a fuzzy red wig, a yellow shirt and baggy checked dungarees.

Sadie wore a bright-blue leotard and silver tights. She had a white face with a big red nose and a crooked painted smile. She wore a backpack and Flame was inside, safe from the milling crowds that lined the pavements, and hidden from his enemies.

'Are you enjoying this?' Lena shouted above the band down to Sadie.

'It's fantastic! I love it!' she yelled

back. 'Isn't it brilliant, Jenny?'

Jenny nodded, her eyes shining. She pointed at the crowd. 'Look, there's my mum and dad. They're with your parents!'

'Hi, Mum! Hi, Dad!' Sadie and Jenny chorused and waved.

The crowds cheered and clapped as the parade passed by. There was a ripple of laughter as a clown on stilts blew a loud hooter.

The carnival parade poured through the park gates with a stream of people following behind it. Strings of coloured lights and spotlights made the park seem magical.

The Tomanis' float came to a halt beside the makeshift circus ring and Lena and her family began getting ready for their evening performance.

'Back soon!' Jenny had an attack of nerves and ran off to find a loo.

Sadie had butterflies in her stomach too. It was almost time for her and Jenny to do their act. She took off her backpack and opened it for a quick word with Flame.

He wasn't inside.

'Flame? Where are you?' Sadie hissed.

As she remembered the only other time he had gone missing, a horrible suspicion crept over her.

Suddenly she glimpsed two lean, dark shapes under a parked lorry. Cruel eyes seemed to flash in the spotlights trained on the ring.

Sadie gasped and her heart missed a beat. Flame's enemies were here. He would be killed. She had to find him and warn him!

As she dashed between the lorries, there was a bright silver flash and a cloud of sparkles. Sadie saw Flame as a magnificent young white lion standing there. This time, there was an older, grey lion alongside him.

Flame turned and looked at Sadie. His calm emerald eyes were gentle.

'Take care. Be well,' he said in a deep velvety growl.

Tears pricked Sadie's eyes. Her chest ached so much she could hardly breathe. 'Goodbye. I'll never forget you,' she croaked.

There was a final flash. Flame and the grey lion had gone.

With a shriek of rage the dark shapes disappeared too.

Sadie stood there. The cheerful noise of the carnival went on around her, but she didn't hear it. She was going to miss Flame dreadfully. But then Sadie realized how proud she felt to have been his friend. She would always have the memories of their time together.

'Sadie?' called Jenny's voice. 'We're on in a minute.'

Sadie wiped her eyes. 'Coming!' she called, as she ran out to meet her friend.

Jenny stared at her tear-streaked face. 'What's happened?'

'Flame's owner turned up and has taken him home,' Sadie improvised hastily. 'I knew he couldn't stay forever. He was a stray, after all.'

'Oh, what a shame. You poor thing. You must be so upset.' Jenny put her arm round Sadie. 'We don't have to do our act, if you'd rather not. I'd understand.'

'After all our hard work? Are you kidding?' Sadie felt the excitement pushing through her sadness as she grabbed Jenny's hand and ran towards the circus ring.

Win a Magic Kitten goody bag!

An urgent and secret message has been left for Flame
from his own world, where his evil uncle is
still hunting for him.

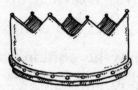

Two words from the message can be found in royal lion
crowns hidden in *Moonlight Mischief* and *A Circus Wish*.
Find the hidden words and put them together to complete
the message. Send it in to us and each month we will
put every correct message in a draw and pick out one lucky
winner who will receive a purrfect Magic Kitten gift!

Send your secret message, name and address on a postcard to:
Magic Kitten Competition
Puffin Books
80 Strand
London WC2R 0RL

Hurry, Flame needs your help!

Good luck!

puffin.co.uk

Visit:
penguin.co.uk/static/cs/uk/0/competition/terms.html
for full terms and conditions